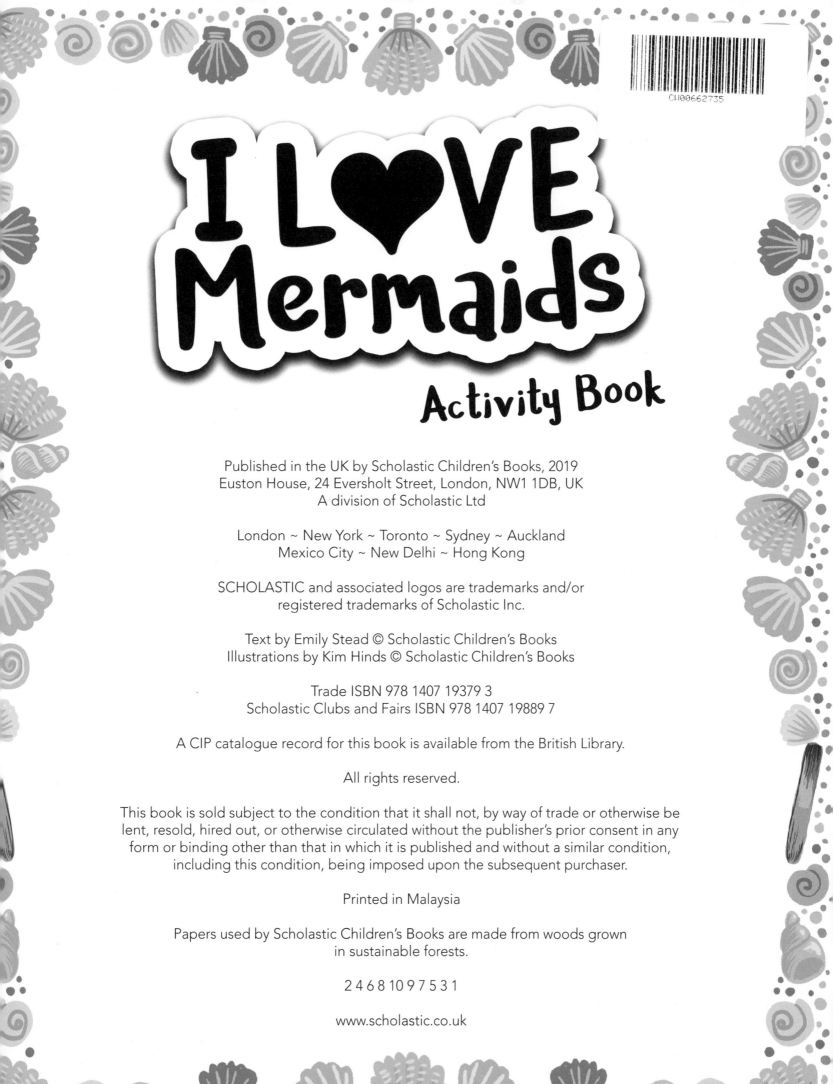

I L♥VE Mermaids

Activity Book

Published in the UK by Scholastic Children's Books, 2019
Euston House, 24 Eversholt Street, London, NW1 1DB, UK
A division of Scholastic Ltd

London ~ New York ~ Toronto ~ Sydney ~ Auckland
Mexico City ~ New Delhi ~ Hong Kong

SCHOLASTIC and associated logos are trademarks and/or
registered trademarks of Scholastic Inc.

Text by Emily Stead © Scholastic Children's Books
Illustrations by Kim Hinds © Scholastic Children's Books

Trade ISBN 978 1407 19379 3
Scholastic Clubs and Fairs ISBN 978 1407 19889 7

Printed in Malaysia

Papers used by Scholastic Children's Books are made from woods grown
in sustainable forests.

2 4 6 8 10 9 7 5 3 1

www.scholastic.co.uk

Meet a Magical Family

Draw lines to match each member of this fishy family to their shadow.

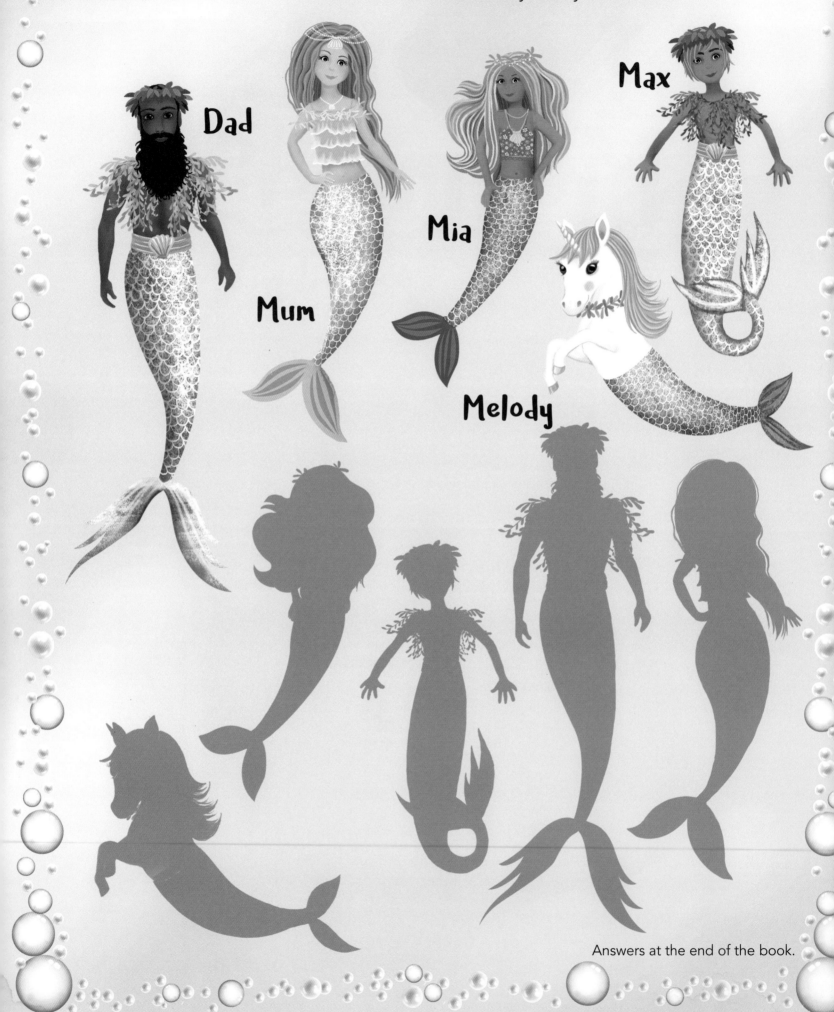

Dad

Mum

Mia

Max

Melody

Answers at the end of the book.

Make a Splash!

Help Megan the mermaid swim through the coral reef to collect an undersea treasure.

Start

Finish

Heads and Tails

Using your stickers, match heads and tails to make some magical creatures below. Then think of a name for each character!

Name:

Name:

Name:

Name:

Name:

Special Sight

Some very special visitors are at the beach today. Help them put the picture back together in the right order! Number one has been done for you.

A   B   C   D   E

1. E   2. ◯   3. ◯   4. ◯   5. ◯

Answers at the end of the book.

Frosty Swim

Join the dots to reveal an Arctic animal enjoying a morning swim!
Add some more fishy friends for him to play with.

If I Were a Mermaid

Imagine you were a mermaid! Write all about your life in the ocean waves below.

My name would be: ....

My hair colour would be:
- ☐ sun-kissed blonde
- ☐ coral pink
- ☐ rainbow shades
- ☐ my choice: ....

My scales would be:
- ☐ sparkly silver
- ☐ ocean blue
- ☐ shimmering rainbow
- ☐ my choice: ....

I would be friends with:
- ☐ narwhals
- ☐ dolphins
- ☐ mermicorns
- ☐ my choice: ....

My favourite things to do would be:
- ☐ singing
- ☐ diving
- ☐ swimming
- ☐ my choice: ....

Making Waves

Dive under the sea to meet a merry mermaid!
Colour her in using the colour code to help you.

You could even add in some shells and starfish!

1 pink

2 purple

3 yellow

4 blue

5 green

6 orange

7 brown

Under the Sea

Use your stickers to create the perfect paradise below the waves for your magical mermaid friends!

Seaside Snacks

Draw lines to give these mermaids a tasty treat to eat. Choose carefully –
each mermaid's favourite food matches the colour of her hair.

Message in a Bottle

A secret mermaid message has washed up on the shore!
Use the code to help you work out what it says.

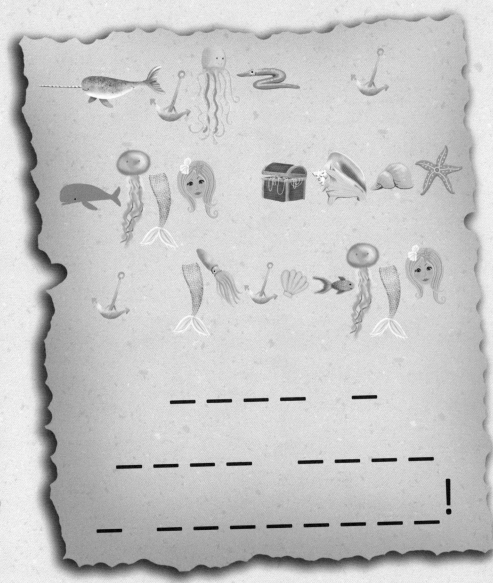

__ __ __ __ __

__ __ __ __ __ __

__ __ __ __ __ __ !

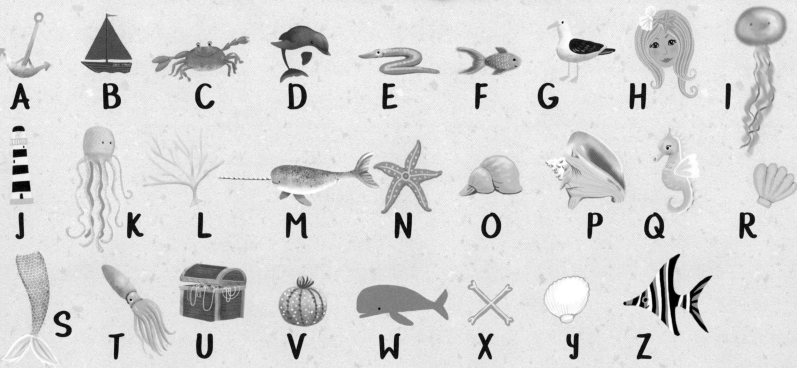

A	B	C	D	E	F	G	H	I

J	K	L	M	N	O	P	Q	R

S	T	U	V	W	X	Y	Z

Answers at the end of the book.

Perfect Party

Molly and her merfolk friends are having a mer-mazing time making music!
Circle 11 differences between the pictures.

Ocean Friends

Use the clues below to help you write the words in the crossword grid. Some of the friends are real, while some are legendary!

DOWN

1. A creature that is half mermaid and half unicorn.
2. A miniature horse that lives in the sea.
3. A magical male with a fishy tail.
5. A mythical horse with a healing horn.
8. This soft sea creature has eight arms in all.

ACROSS

3. A fishtailed siren of the sea.
4. This scuttling sea creature has a hard shell.
6. A gleaming treasure of the sea.
7. A wonderful whale with a twisted tusk.

Answers at the end of the book.

Magical Makeover

Mia the mermaid is ready for her makeover, but some of her things are missing.
Find the stickers of the things she needs and place them in the picture.

Now unscramble the letters to discover Mia's three favourite things.

 R A T A I _ _ _ _ _

○○○○ L A C K E N E C _ _ _ _ _ _ _ _

 M U F E R P E _ _ _ _ _ _ _

Answers at the end of the book.

These are the stickers for the
'Heads and Tails' activity.

These are the stickers for the 'Treasure Triangle' activity.

These are the stickers for the 'Magical Makeover' activity.

These are the stickers for the 'Triton's Test' activity.

These are the stickers for the 'Mermaid Greeting' activity.

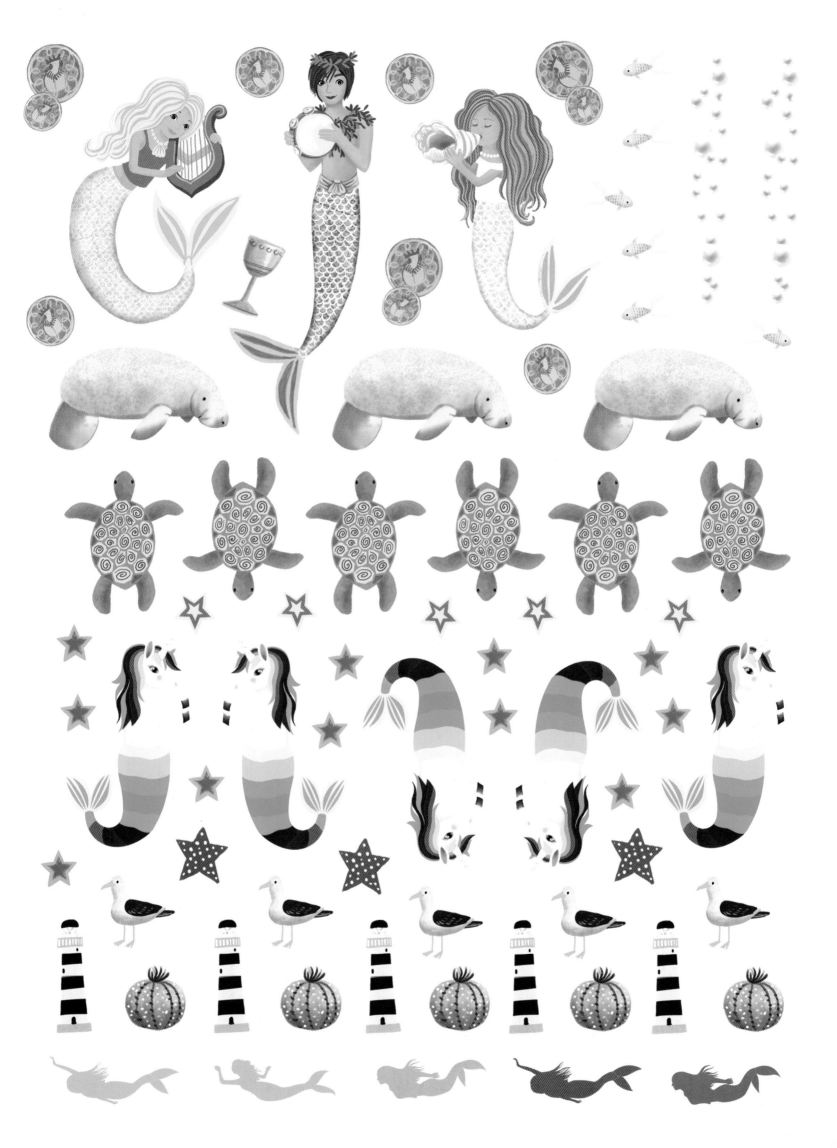

These are the stickers for the 'Picture Puzzles' activity.

These are the stickers for the 'Under the Sea' activity.

These are the stickers for the 'Frosty Swim' activity.

Triton's Test

Triton has set you a tricky quiz! Find the right stickers to answer the questions all about mermaids. Answer true or false each time, then place the correct sticker.

2. The word 'mermaid' means 'woman of the sea'.

☐ True
☐ False

1. Creatures called sea cows or manatees were often mistaken for mermaids.

☐ True
☐ False

3. Some people believe that the gemstone garnet is made from mermaids' tears.

☐ True ☐ False

4. It was considered bad luck for a sailor at sea to spot a mermaid.

☐ True
☐ False

5. The original fairy tale The Little Mermaid by Hans Christian Andersen did not have a happy ending.

☐ True ☐ False

6. Mermaids can only live in freshwater pools.

☐ True
☐ False

7. A mermaid's tail moves up and down like a dolphin's, rather than from side to side.

☐ True ☐ False

8. Some stories claim that mermaids can predict the future.

☐ True
☐ False

Answers at the end of the book.

How to Draw a Mermaid

Follow these simple steps to draw a friendly mermaid.

Treasure Tangle

Add the missing treasure stickers, then follow the lines to help each mermaid swim to find her prize.

Double Bubble

Trace over the lines to help this mermicorn make a friend.
Then colour in the picture.

Sea Search

Find ten words all about mermaids in the word search below. The words read forwards, down and up.

```
              Q  U  N  A
           F  L  I  P  P  E  R  U
        F  Y  C  P  B  W  T  R  T  U  X  N
     T  I  D  M  O  Y  U  A  K  I  F  I  N  B
  P  I  P  M  E  R  M  A  I  D  H  J  R  P  D  I
  F  A  F  Y  R  H  E  Z  L  H  U  C  S  M  E  O
  H  R  H  K  M  S  R  V  K  L  Q  D  H  U  Z  L
  A  J  G  A  C  M  U  T  N  J  D  E  R  M
  T  T  V  N  U  I  Q  J  H  B  I  L  Y
     I  U  W  S  C  A  L  E  S  W  L  J
     Y  D  R  O  J  P  K  L  C  S
        S  I  R  E  N  T  K  H
        K  X  N  W  V  S  Y  I
           J  U  F  L  I  P
           F  A  B  U
              V  E
```

TIARA   SCALES   TAIL   FLIPPER   SIREN   SHELLS

FIN   MERMAID   MERMAN   MERMICORN

Picture Puzzles

Look carefully at these picture patterns, then add the missing stickers to complete each row.

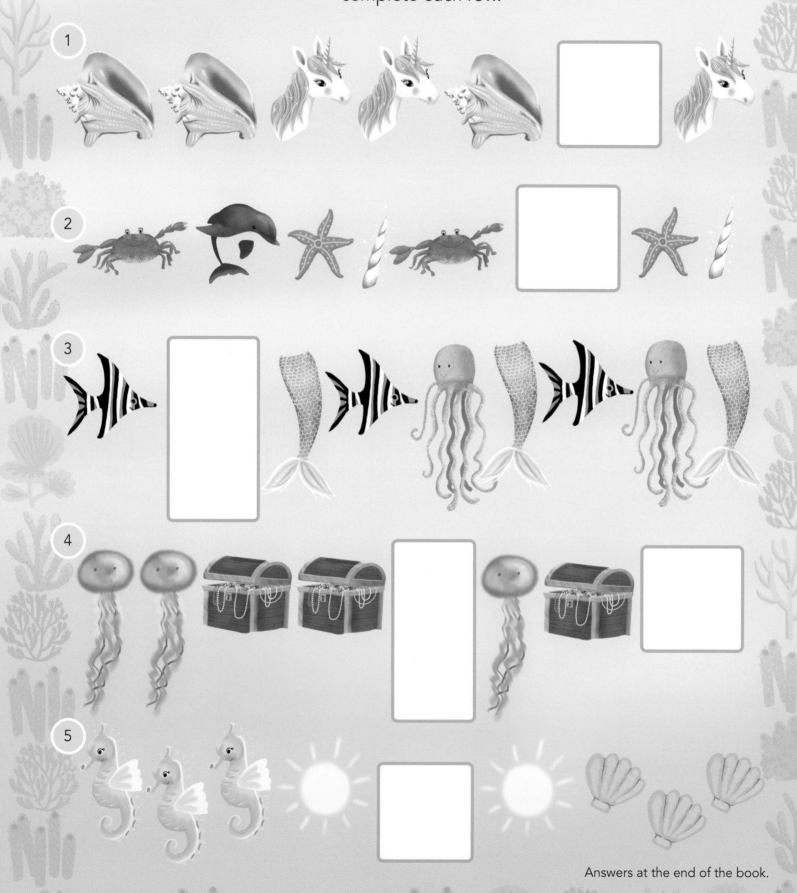

Pretty Prize

Colour in each shape with a dot to discover a mermaid's hidden treasure!

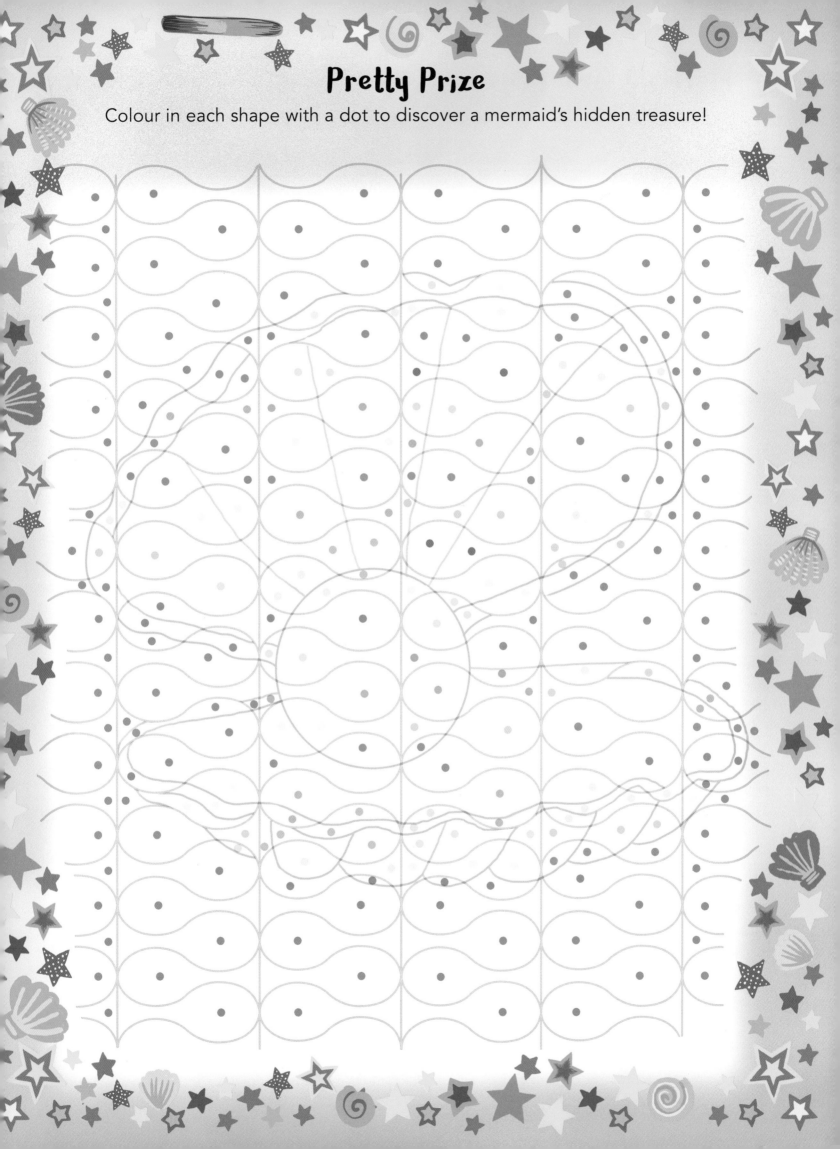

Mermaid Greetings

Cut out the postcards on the next page, then choose four friends who would love to receive a mermaid message! Add stickers to match the shapes below.

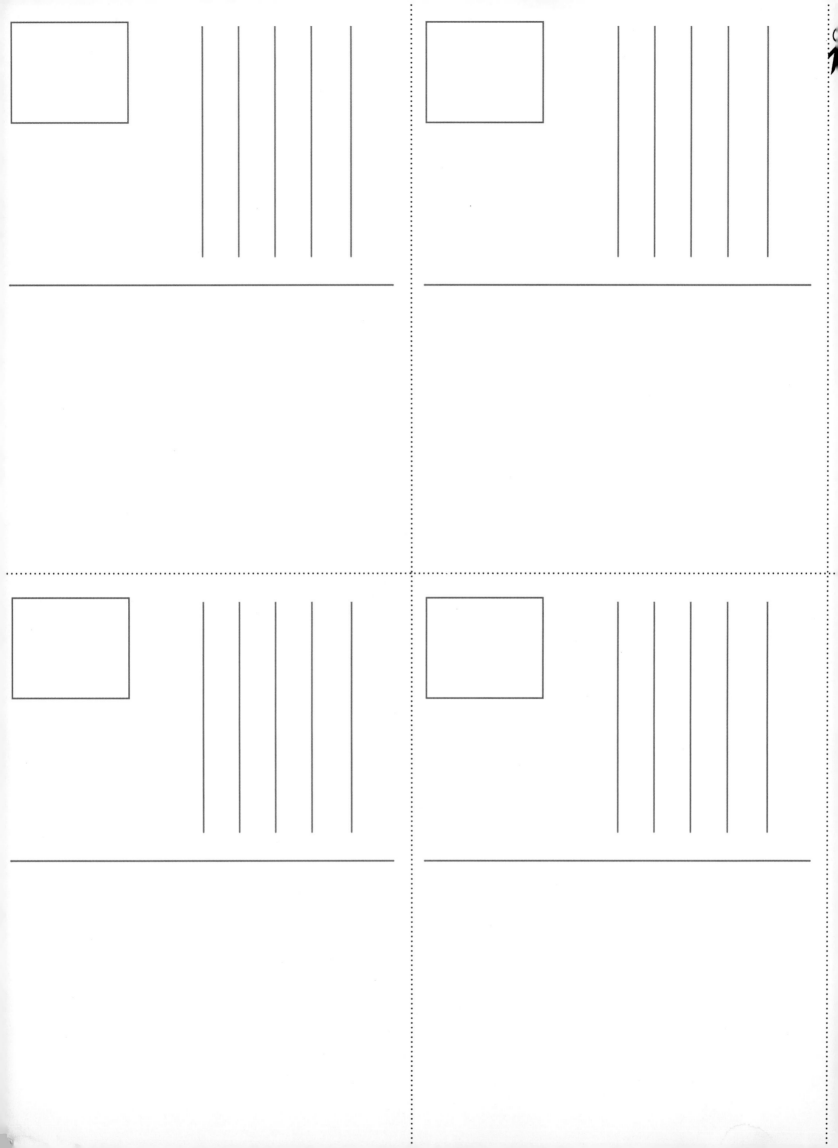

Mermaid Dreams

What do mermaids dream of? Meeting a mermicorn or walking on land? Decide for yourself by drawing this mermaid's dream in the bubble.

Sunshine Fun

Time to enjoy the summer! Which of these close-ups can you see in the main picture? Cross out the detail you can't see.

Answers at the end of the book.

Diving Deep

Finish doodling some pretty patterns on these mermicorns' tails.

My Mermicorn Name

Would you like to make friends with a magical mermicorn?
Follow the instructions to reveal your mermicorn's name.

First, look for the month in which you were born...

January – Crystal

February – Bubbles

March – Coral

April – Melody

May – Calypso

June – Ariel

July – Isla

August – Sapphire

September – Laguna

October – Marina

November – Ocean

December – Pearl

Now find the day on which you were born...

1 – Sky Soarer

2 – Winter Belle

3 – the Princess

4 – Seaweed Scent

5 – Rainbow Sparkle

6 – Shiny Flipper

7 – Cloud Prancer

8 – Honey Love

9 – Shimmer Tail

10 – Bright Eyes

11 – Moonbeam Mane

12 – Summer Dream

13 – Sparkly Scales

14 – Giddy Gallop

15 – Lucky Fin

16 – Wave Whisperer

17 – Fluffy Cloud

18 – Sugar Socks

19 – Dreamer

20 – Happy Hooves

21 – Glitter Fin

22 – Splashy Tail

23 – Moonlit Glow

24 – Star Dust

25 – Blossom Breeze

26 – Fancy Face

27 – Wave Dancer

28 – Sunshine Ray

29 – Sugar Plum

30 – Sweet Cheeks

31 – Twinkle Toes

Write the name of your fantastic friend here:

_____

_____

_____

Cuddle Time

Copy these snuggly friends into the grid below, then colour them in.

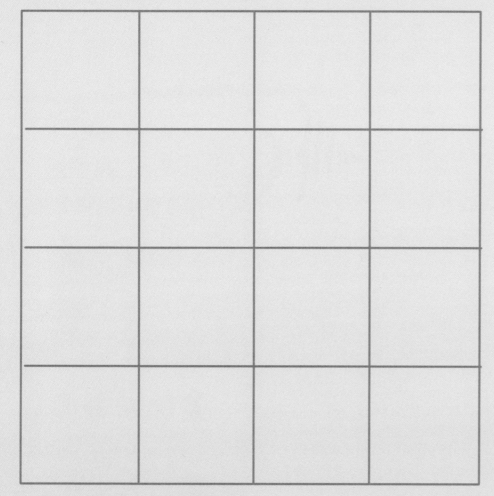

Meet a Magical Family

Make a Splash!

Special Sight

1.E 2.C 3. B 4. D 5.A

Seaside Snacks

Answers

Message in a Bottle

The message reads:
MAKE A WISH UPON
A STARFISH!

Perfect Party

Ocean Friends

Across and Down crossword:

- 1 DOWN: MERMICORN
- 2 DOWN: SEAHORSE
- 3 ACROSS: MERMAID / 3 DOWN: MERMAN
- 4 ACROSS: CRAB
- 5 DOWN: UNICORN
- 6 ACROSS: PEARL
- 7 ACROSS: NARWHAL
- 8 DOWN: OCTOPUS

Magical Makeover

1. TIARA, 2. NECKLACE
3. PERFUME.

Triton's Test

1. true, 2. true, 3. false – though some believe aquamarine is made from mermaids' tears, 4. true, 5. true, 6. false – mermaids mostly live in saltwater, though are said to live in freshwater lakes too, 7. this is said to be true, 8. this is said to be true.

Treasure Tangle

1. D, 2. B, 3. A, 4 C

Sea Search

Word search containing: FLIPPER, TIARA, FIN, MERMAID, SHELLS, SCALES, SIREN

```
        Q U N A
      F L I P P E R U
    F Y C P B W T R T U X N
  T I D M O Y U A K I F I N B
P I P F Y R H E Z L H U C S M E O
F A F Y R H E Z L H U C S H U Z L
H R H K M S R V K L Q D E L R Y M
  A J G A C M U T N J D E L L
  T T V N U I Q J H B I L L J
  I U W S C A L E S W L S
  Y D R O J P K L C S
    S I R E N T K H
    K X N W V S Y I
    J U F L I P
    F A B U
    V E
```

Picture Puzzles

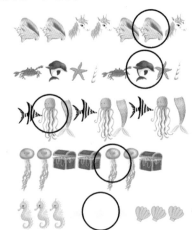

Sunshine Fun